Duck
and his friends

Notes for Parents

This is a book to share with a young child who is beginning to talk. At this stage of their development, children need lots of opportunities to learn new words and phrases, and lots of practice using those they already know in different ways and situations. Each picture in this book is designed to stimulate discussion about what Duck is doing and about the things around him. There are objects to name and things to spot or count. The text on each page is intended only as a starting point for wider conversation.

Very young children have to learn that a book has a sequence and that, by starting at the beginning and turning the pages one by one, they can follow this sequence to find out what happens next. The pictures in this book tell a short, very simple story for children who are just ready to learn this important new skill.

Duck
and his friends

Jenny Tyler and Philip Hawthorn
Illustrated by Stephen Cartwright

Consultant: Betty Root
Edited by Heather Amery

Here's Duck who has a brand new hat,
He hears a rustle, up pops Cat.

They leap and jump and hop so high,
To try and catch a butterfly.

They're very hot, but help is near,
It's Frog who has a bright idea.

Both Duck and Frog enjoy a swim,
But Cat's not sure if she'll go in.

They want some lunch, but what to do?
Then peeping Piglet says, "Er ... Boo!"

He says, "Tuck in, it's only swill,
I hope it doesn't make you ill."

Then Duck and Piglet, Frog and Cat
Find cheeky Monkey with Duck's hat.

And now the fun and games begin,
They all play football, guess who'll win.

"My tummy's rumbling now," croaks Frog,
"It must be time for tea," barks Dog.

They have a scrummy picnic scoff,
While Piglet grunts and dozes off.

His friends are hiding round about,
Duck needs your help to seek them out.
(So when you spot each one, just shout!)

First published in 1987. This enlarged edition first published in 1992. Usborne Publishing Ltd. Usborne House, 83-85 Saffron Hill, London ECIN 8RT. Copyright © Usborne Publishing Ltd. 1992